Alfred A. Knopf
New York

ROOM FOR BEAR

Ciara Gavin

One spring, Bear came to visit and never left.

Life with his duck family suited him perfectly.
He was sure he belonged.

But duck houses were not built with bears in mind.

Things were always a little crowded.

And so the search for a perfect home began.

It wasn't easy.

What suited Bear didn't suit the ducks.

And what suited the ducks didn't suit Bear.

They all returned to their
home by the lake.

But Bear began to worry. Maybe he and his family *didn't* fit together.

"I'm a nuisance," he thought. "I will go and find my own home."

"Nothing feels right without Bear," the ducks said.

Bear found a perfect cave. But somehow
it didn't feel like home.

"Quack, quack," he whispered to himself.

Bear thought of all the things he missed about the ducks.

Then Bear had an idea. He got to work.

When he was finished, Bear went to find the ducks.

"Nothing felt right without you, Bear," they said.

"I missed you all very much," said Bear.
"Come and see. I have a surprise for you."

Bear had built the ducks a new house.
Now they would have everything they needed.

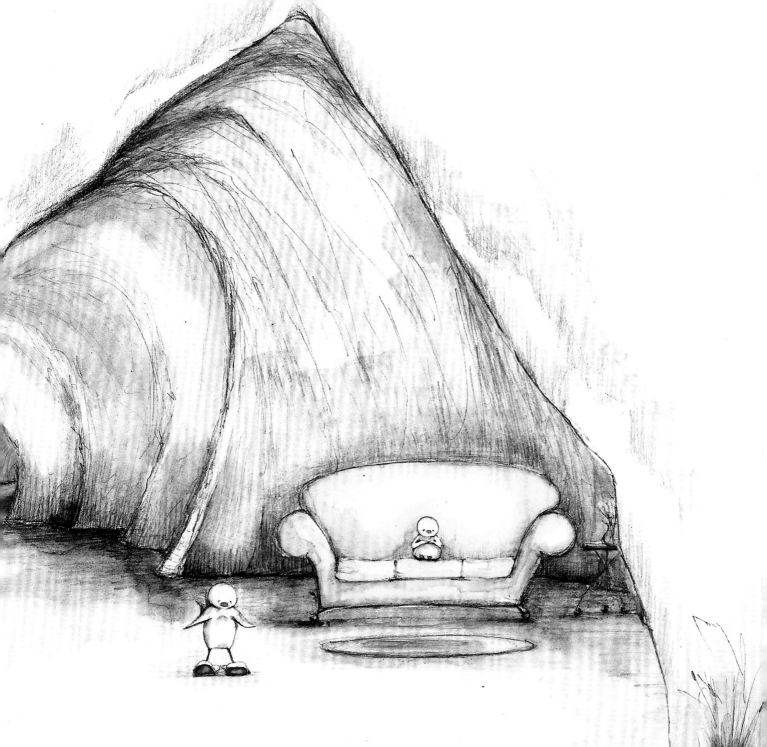

Most importantly, they would
have each other.

Before long, they settled into their new home.
And as it turned out, ducks and bears were not
such an odd match.

In fact, they were a perfect fit.

THIS IS A BORZOI BOOK PUBLISHED BY ALFRED A. KNOPF

Copyright © 2015 by Ciara Gavin

All rights reserved. Published in the United States by Alfred A. Knopf, an imprint of Random House

Children's Books, a division of Random House LLC, a Penguin Random House Company, New York.

Knopf, Borzoi Books, and the colophon are registered trademarks of Random House LLC.

Visit us on the Web! randomhouse.com/kids

Educators and librarians, for a variety of teaching tools, visit us at RHTeachersLibrarians.com

Library of Congress Cataloging-in-Publication Data

Gavin, Ciara, author, illustrator.

Room for Bear / Ciara Gavin. — First edition.

   p. cm.

Summary: Bear and a family of ducks try to find the perfect home to share, but what suits the bear

does not suit the ducks, and what suits the ducks does not suit Bear.

ISBN 978-0-385-75473-6 (trade) — ISBN 978-0-385-75474-3 (lib. bdg.) — ISBN 978-0-385-75475-0 (ebook)

[1. Dwellings—Fiction. 2. Size—Fiction. 3. Bears—Fiction. 4. Ducks—Fiction.] I. Title.

PZ7.G2354Roo 2015   [E]—dc23 2013040226

The illustrations in this book were created using watercolor and pencil.

MANUFACTURED IN CHINA

March 2015 10 9 8 7 6 5 4 3 2 1 First Edition

Random House Children's Books supports the First Amendment and celebrates the right to read.